Time for Breakfast!

by Tawnya Dubois
illustrated by Laura Gibbons Nikiel

HOUGHTON MIFFLIN   BOSTON

Printed in India

ISBN-13: 978-0-547-02023-5
ISBN-10: 0-547-02023-6

3 4 5 6 7 8 9 0940 15 14 13 12 11 10

eggs

See the eggs.

toaster

toast

See the toast.

juice

See the juice.

pancakes

See the pancakes.

See the breakfast!

Responding

Cause and Effect This story is about a family of rabbits. Tell what happens. Tell why it happens. Make a chart.

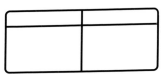

Talk About It

Text to Self Have you ever made something special for your parents? Draw a picture of it. Then tell about your picture.

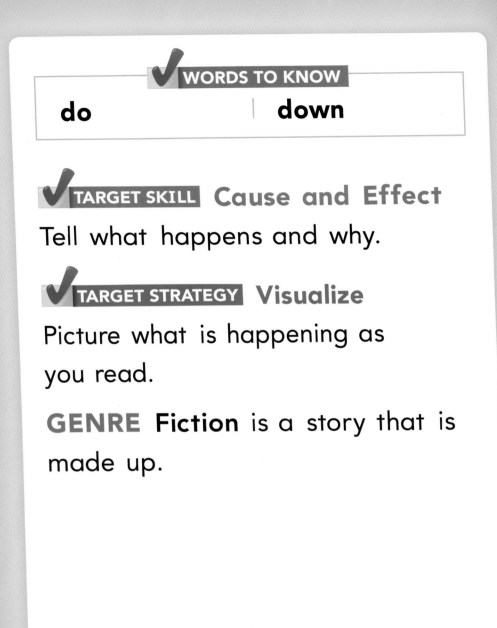

✓ **WORDS TO KNOW**

do | **down**

✓ **TARGET SKILL** Cause and Effect
Tell what happens and why.

✓ **TARGET STRATEGY** Visualize
Picture what is happening as
you read.

GENRE Fiction is a story that is
made up.